HEROES OF BEESVILLE

by Coach John Wooden

with Steve Jamison
and Bonnie Graves

Illustrated by
Susan F. Cornelison

Perfection Learning®

Editorial Director: Susan C. Thies
Design Director: Randy Messer
Cover Design: Tobi Cunningham

For information, contact
Perfection Learning® Corporation
1000 North Second Avenue, P.O. Box 500
Logan, Iowa 51546-0500
Phone: 1-800-831-4190
Fax: 1-800-543-2745
perfectionlearning.com

1 2 3 4 5 6 PP 11 10 09 08 07 06

Paperback ISBN 0-7891-6853-7
Reinforced Library Binding ISBN 0-7569-6408-3

CONTENTS

CHAPTER 1

Problems

"Open House is only three weeks away,"
Mr. Wooden told the class. "Decide on your
group projects and then get started. Pronto!"

Inch and Miles exchanged glances. Mr.
Wooden had grouped them with Pepper and
Lily. Their projects had to show something the
class had been studying.

"Please meet with your group and decide

what your project will be," Mr. Wooden told them. "Remember, it will take cooperation."

Inch and Miles raced to a table by the windows where Pepper and Lily already sat. Pepper was wearing his carpenter's belt. All sorts of tools hung from the loops on the belt. Lily clutched a notebook with pictures of movie stars on it. In front of her sat her lunch box with ballerinas dancing all over it.

"So," Miles said with a grin, opening his box of colored pencils. "Let's draw a map of our school!"

"No, way," said Pepper. "Let's build a model spaceship! We've been studying space."

"Boring!" said Lily. "Let's make a play about Día de Los Muertos—Day of the Dead! One with singing and dancing!" She showed them her notebook filled with songs and ideas for plays.

"Yuck!" said Inch. "I think we should identify the animal and insect species in the neighborhood." He showed them the binoculars his mom had given him for his birthday. "Then we could make a diorama. Now that would be a great project!"

Miles groaned. Pepper and Lily did too.

"Yeah, great if you like spying on insects and animals," said Pepper.

"I do," said Inch. Inch was the class bug-and-animal man.

"Well, I like to build things!" said Pepper.

"And I like to act and sing and dance!" said Lily.

"And I like to draw," said Miles.

Inch, Miles, Pepper, and Lily argued loudly about what their project should be until Mr. Wooden blew his whistle.

"Hold on there," Mr. Wooden said, walking over to their table. "What's going on?" He put his hands on his hips and frowned at the four.

"We can't agree on a project," Miles said. "We all want to do something different."

"Yeah," said Inch. "Like the things we like to do and are good at."

"Looks like none of you is very good at agreeing," Mr. Wooden said. "Are you going to be the only group with NO project for Open House?"

Inch, Miles, Pepper, and Lily stared at one another. They knew they had a problem. A big one.

Mr. Wooden shook his head. "Have you forgotten the blocks on the Pyramid of Success that will help you with this project?"

"Not all of them," Miles said, looking over at Inch. Miles remembered a few of the ideas on the Pyramid of Success, like hard work—and being enthusiastic. But he didn't think either of those was going to help with the problem his group had now.

Inch stared at the whistle that dangled on a cord around Mr. Wooden's neck. The silver whistle glistened in the sunlight that shone through the classroom windows. The magic silver whistle. Inch cleared his throat.

"Mr. Wooden, may we borrow your silver whistle?" Inch asked.

"Again?"

"Please!" Inch and Miles said.

"We don't want to be the only group without a project," said Miles.

"Right-o," said Lily. "That would be embarrassing."

"Yeah," said Pepper.

"My mother would ground me," said Inch.

Mr. Wooden rubbed his chin. "Well, maybe the whistle might help. But I warn you. Be careful with it—very careful. This whistle cannot be replaced."

"Yes, sir. We'll be careful," Miles said.

"Very careful," Inch added. "Won't we, Pepper and Lily?"

Pepper and Lily nodded. "Right-o," said Lily.

Mr. Wooden took the whistle from around his neck and gave it to Miles. Miles lifted the whistle to his mouth.

"No!" exclaimed Mr. Wooden. "Not here! Take it to the edge of the school yard. And remember, take good care of that whistle."

CHAPTER 2

Stuck

Inch, Miles, Pepper, and Lily raced to
the edge of the school yard. Miles wore Mr.
Wooden's silver whistle around his neck. In his
hand he carried his box of colored pencils.

Lily had her song-and-dance notebook and
her lunch box with the dancing ballerinas.

Pepper wore his carpenter's belt.

Inch wore his binoculars.

"OK, guys. Ready?" Miles said. "Huddle."

The foursome made a small circle like a
football huddle. Then Miles blew the whistle.

Suddenly the school yard disappeared. Inch, Miles, Pepper, and Lily floated through creamy cotton clouds.

"Hey, this is cool!" said Pepper.

Then they heard strange sounds like thunder in a bottle, rain in a teakettle, and lightning cracking upside down and sideways.

"Yikes!" said Lily. "What's happening?"

Inch, Miles, Pepper, and Lily closed their eyes and plugged their ears. When they opened their eyes again, they were standing in a meadow thick with clover.

"Where are we?" Lily asked.

"Don't know," said Miles. He looked around. The sun shone brightly. The meadow was the size of a football field. Woods surrounded the meadow—woods with leafy trees and tall pines. Miles stretched and took a deep breath of the warm, scented air.

"Miles," Inch said. "I think we've been here before . . . on our first adventure with the silver whistle."

"I think you're right, Inch."

"Weird," said Lily. "It's summer here, not fall like at school . . . and it's hot!"

"Smells good too," Miles said, taking another deep breath.

"Well, I don't know how being in a meadow in the middle of a woods is going to help us with our project!" Pepper said. "Blow that whistle again and get us out of here!"

A buzzing sound made the foursome turn around. A bee hovered above them.

"Betty!" Inch and Miles said.

"Hey," the bee said. "You two again . . . and you brought friends this time. I suppose you came for honey."

"Yum," said Lily. "I love honey."

"Actually," Miles said, "we have a problem and we're looking for help. We need to do a project for Open House at our school. I want to draw a map of our school. Pepper wants to make a model spaceship."

"I want to do a play," Lily said. "With singing and dancing."

"And I want to make an insect-and-animal diorama," said Inch.

"Sorry guys, we bees make honey, not maps, spaceships, plays, or dioramas. Can't help you," Betty said.

"Told you!" Pepper said to Miles. "Blow that whistle again."

"Could we eat a little honey first?" asked Lily.

"No!" said Pepper. "Blow the whistle, Miles."

Miles blew the silver whistle. Again they

floated through clouds and heard loud noises,
but when they opened their eyes, they stood in
exactly the same spot—a field of clover.

"Maybe you didn't blow hard enough,"
Inch told Miles. "Try again."

"Huddle, guys," Miles said.

"Right-o," said Lily.

The four classmates huddled together. Then Miles blew the whistle with all the breath he could muster. They floated through clouds and heard loud noises, but when they opened their eyes again, they were back in the same spot.

Miles blew the whistle three more times and exactly the same thing happened.

"I think the whistle's broken," Miles said with a sigh.

"Does that mean we're stuck here?" Inch asked.

"Good thing I'm wearing my carpenter's belt!" Pepper commented. "We might have to build a spaceship to get us back to school!"

Lily groaned. "Yeah, right-o, Pepper," she said. "Well, at least we have something to eat—honey."

Inch sighed. "I can't eat sweets before dinner."

Inch, Miles, Pepper, and Lily began arguing about what they were going to do and how they were going to get out of Beesville. They argued until they were so tired they lay down in the clover, but they couldn't fall asleep. They were too worried and afraid.

How were they going to get out of Beesville? *Would* they get out?

CHAPTER 3

Trouble in Beesville

"Hey!" Betty Bee said. "You guys still here? You can't lie around in the clover! No one's idle in Beesville. Summer's almost over. We've got to make honey—lots of it—enough for winter."

"And how is that *our* problem?" Pepper asked.

"Quit the attitude," Miles told Pepper. "We have a problem, too, don't forget."

"Yeah, all because of you and that stupid whistle!" Pepper said.

"Stop it!" said Inch.

"Yeah, Pepper," said Lily. "We're here. We might as well help Betty."

"Lily's right," Miles said. "Betty, how can we help?"

"Well, I'm not sure you can. We bees have a problem—a life-and-death problem."

"Wow!" said Inch. "That sounds bad. What is it?"

"Ima Skunk," Betty said.

Inch, Miles, Lily, and even Pepper giggled.

"You don't look like a skunk. You look like a bee," said Pepper with a smile.

Betty looked confused. Then she laughed too. "No, no. Ima is a skunk, a real one . . . and a thief! Twice this summer she has found our hive and taken our honey. If she steals again, we won't have enough honey for winter. The colony will be done for."

21

Lily's stomach grumbled because of all the talk about honey. "But we don't know how to make honey," Lily said.

"So what do you know how to do?" Betty asked. "Everyone's good at something!"

Inch, Miles, Pepper, and Lily glanced at each other.

"I'm pretty good at drawing," Miles said.

"I know a lot about animals and bugs," said Inch.

"I'm good at building things," said Pepper. He stood a little taller, showing off his carpenter's belt with all the tools.

"I'm good at acting, singing, and dancing," said Lily, doing a little dance.

Betty buzzed in circles above the clover. When she came back she said, "Do you think you could use any of those talents to help us with Ima Skunk?"

Miles motioned for Inch, Pepper, and Lily to get into a huddle. "Listen, guys," Miles said. "Let's put our heads together and see if we can figure out a way to help Betty. What do you say?"

"OK," Pepper said. "We're stuck here, so we might as well."

"Right-o," said Lily. "Maybe Betty will give us some honey."

Inch hung his head.

"What's the matter, Inch?" Miles asked.

"What if we never get home? They'll put our faces on milk cartons. That would really make my mom cry!" Inch said sadly.

"Don't worry, Inch," said Miles. "We're in this together. We'll figure a way out."

Lily put her arm around Inch. "We'll find a way to get back to school," she told Inch. Then she looked at Betty. "If we promise to help you with Ima Skunk, can we have a little honey?"

"Of course!" said Betty.

"How 'bout it, guys?" Lily said. "Put it there?" Lily stuck out her hand.

First Miles put his hand on top of Lily's, then Inch, and finally Pepper.

"We have two big problems to solve," Miles said. "Helping the bees protect their honey supply AND getting back to school."

"Wrong," said Pepper. "We have a third problem—our Open House project. We need one . . . if we ever get back to school, that is."

CHAPTER 4

What to Do?

"Well," said Betty. "Gotta buzz."

As Betty flitted away to join the other bees in collecting nectar to make into honey, Inch called, "Do you know where Ima Skunk's den is?"

Betty pointed west. "Over there. Somewhere in those woods west of the meadow."

"And the hive with your honeycomb?" Inch asked.

"There," said Betty, pointing east. "Where

those bees are heading. The old oak tree in the woods east of the meadow."

"We'll try our best to help you out," Inch said.

"Thanks," said Betty. "And good luck," she called as she buzzed away. "We bees are counting on you!"

"OK," Miles said, draping his arm over his buddy Inch. "You're the one who can help us now. You're the animal expert. Tell us all you know about skunks."

"You tell me and I'll write it down," offered Lily. She opened her writing notebook, the one where she jotted down her ideas for songs and plays.

"Tell us everything you can think of, Inch," said Miles. "You never know what might help."

Inch didn't have to think for long. Lily wrote furiously.

Skunks

Spray stinky liquid when fear danger.

Stamp and hiss before spraying.

Spray up to 12 feet.

Body about 13 to 18 inches long.

Two white stripes that make a V.

Live in an underground den lined with dry leaves.

Asleep in the day and awake at night.

Eat insects, small rodents, and just about anything.

"Wow!" said Lily, reading over Inch's list. "You're smart!"

Inch blushed. "Not really," he said. "I just read a lot about animals and bugs."

"Big deal," said Pepper. "I don't see how any of that is going to help us."

"How can we catch Ima Skunk," Miles said, "if we don't know anything about skunks?"

"Right-o!" said Lily, pointing to Inch's list. "Like since skunks sleep in the day, Ima must be stealing at night!" Lily shouted.

"Good thinking!" Miles said.

"So, how do we keep her from doing that?" Pepper said. "It's dark at night. We can't even see her!"

"Inch can," Miles said. "He's got great eyes . . . and those binoculars."

Pepper laughed. "Look at Inch! He's the shortest of all of us. Even if he has super eyes and powerful binoculars, how's he going to spot a skunk in all this clover?"

Inch hung his head. "Pepper's right. This meadow's huge and the clover is thick. I can't see through it, even with my binoculars."

"We have to figure out a way to keep Ima from stealing the honey. We promised Betty," Lily said. "Look at Inch's list again and THINK!"

They heard a buzzing sound. Betty was flying toward them.

"Something I forgot to tell you. Ima always strikes when there's a full moon."

"Uh-oh," said Inch.

"What's the matter?" asked Miles.

"Tonight," said Inch. "There's a full moon tonight!"

CHAPTER 5

The Plan

"That means we have to work fast," Miles
said. He took a blue pencil from his pencil
box and began drawing a map. With a green
pencil, he drew the meadow with the woods
around it. With a yellow pencil, he marked the
location of the hive in the east woods. He used
a red pencil to mark the possible location of
Ima Skunk's den in the west woods.

"Look at this map and think," said Miles.
"It might help us come up with a plan."

"I know!" Pepper exclaimed. "We can build
a watchtower in the meadow!"

"A watchtower?" Lily asked.

"Yeah, so Inch can see all over the meadow . . . spot the skunk crossing the meadow toward the beehive," Pepper said.

"Hmm," said Miles. "That just might work." He turned to Lily. "Can I borrow a piece of paper from your notebook?"

"Right-o," said Lily. She flipped through pages and pages of songs and snippets of plays until she found a blank page.

Miles sketched a plan for the tower. When he was through, it looked kind of like the Eiffel Tower in France and kind of like a windmill tower on a farm. "Here's the plan," said Miles. "Inch will watch from the tower with his binoculars. When he spots Ima Skunk coming, he will quickly slide down this pole." Miles drew a straight line from the top to the bottom of the tower, smack-dab in the center. "Sliding will be faster than climbing down."

"Great idea!" Inch said. "Then what?"

"Then Pepper and I will run a relay to the beehive. Pepper will run through the meadow halfway to the hive." Miles drew an X in the meadow, halfway between the tower and the beehive. "This is where I'll be waiting. Pepper will tag up with me here, and I'll race to the beehive to warn Betty and the rest of the bees that the skunk is coming."

"What about me?" Lily asked. "What's my job?"

"I know," said Inch. "Entertainment. You can sing to keep me awake! I'll be staying up past my bedtime."

"Right-o, Inch," said Lily. "That's a great idea!"

Pepper took a ruler from his carpenter's belt and started measuring Miles' drawing. "That tower needs to be higher," he said.

Inch looked at the clover-filled meadow. "Pepper is right," he said. "That tower would have to be a lot higher for me to see all over the meadow and into the woods where Ima Skunk's den is."

"But guys!" Lily said. "We don't have time to build a higher tower. Tonight's the full moon. That's when Betty said Ima Skunk will attack."

"Yeah," agreed Pepper, looking at the afternoon sky. The sun had already begun its journey toward sunset. "We've only got a few hours to find some wood and build the tower."

"Well, let's put our heads together and think!" Miles said. "We have to make this tower work! It's our only hope!"

Inch, Miles, Pepper, and Lily flopped down in the clover-filled meadow and thought and thought.

Then Lily got up and started dancing through the meadow.

"What are you doing?" Pepper yelled.

"Dancing helps me think," Lily said.

"Dumb, really dumb," said Pepper.

A little while later, they heard Lily singing as she danced back to them.

"I found something!" she said. "Something that will make the tower work!"

CHAPTER 6

The Tower

Lily led Miles, Inch, and Pepper into the meadow. There in the center a small hill rose. "If we build the tower on top of that mound, then Inch can see all over the meadow and into the woods!" Lily said.

"Excellent!" Inch and Miles said together.

"Wait!" said Pepper. "Where are we going to get lumber?"

Lily grinned. "Follow me, guys!" Lily started singing a song about building the tower as she danced ahead of them. Inch, Miles, and

Pepper followed Lily into the woods. She led them to a partly-built cabin. Next to the cabin stood a pile of weathered lumber.

"Looks like someone was going to build a cabin and then stopped," Miles said.

"Lucky for us," said Pepper. "This lumber should do fine for the tower. But we've got to work fast!"

After an hour of carrying wood to the meadow, Inch, Miles, and Pepper were surprised to see that Lily's pile was the biggest. "Dancing has made my muscles strong, and singing while you work makes it more fun," she told them.

"If you stack the wood into piles by size, that will help," Pepper told them.

"I can hand you the wood too," said Miles.

"Thanks," said Pepper. Then he set to work on the tower with his carpenter tools and nails.

"I'll go gather some berries," said Lily. "I'm starving."

"Bring some back for us!" said Miles.

And off danced Lily, singing.

Inch was resting. He had to be wide awake into the night.

At the top of the small hill at the center of the meadow, Pepper nailed the wood together to make the tower's base. Miles handed him the longest and thickest lumber for the base. As Pepper worked his way up the tower, the tower became narrower. When the tower was about half-built, Lily came dancing back.

"What's that on your face?" Miles asked.

Lily put her hand up to her face. There were blue stains all around her mouth.

"So," said Miles, "did you bring us any berries? Or did you eat them all?"

Lily blushed. She opened her lunch box. Miles looked inside. A handful of round, juicy berries lay inside Lily's lunch box next to the crusts of a sandwich and half a Twinkie.

"You might have shared your lunch," Miles said.

Lily looked down at the ground. "Sorry, dancing makes me so hungry! Have some berries."

Just as Miles was reaching into Lily's lunch box, Pepper yelled, "Help!"

CHAPTER 7

Uh-Oh!

Inch woke up. He and Miles and Lily turned to look at Pepper. He hung from the top rungs of the almost-built tower, clinging to one of the crossbars. There he dangled, his feet flailing.

"Oh, no!" Inch yelled.

Then the tower tilted.

"Hold on!" Miles yelled.

"The tower's going to fall over!" Lily shouted.

At once the three ran toward the tower.

They pushed with all their might on the leaning side, while Pepper dangled high above them.

"Try moving to the other side!" Miles called to Pepper.

"I can't! What if I fall?"

"Pretend you're on the monkey bars!" Lily shouted. "Hand over hand to the other side!"

Pepper lifted one hand, then the other, slowly moving along the crossbar to the other side. Inch, Miles, and Lily pressed with all their might against the bottom of the tower to keep it from tumbling over.

As the three pushed, the tower began to straighten. They looked up at Pepper, still hanging by his hands, but now on the other side of the tower. "I can't hold on any longer!" he shouted.

And then he fell.

Inch, Miles, and Lily raced over to Pepper. "Are you OK?" they asked.

"I don't know," said Pepper. "My right hand hurts." He wiggled his fingers. "But I think I can still hammer. I need to build the platform and put the pole in. That will make the tower more stable."

Inch and Miles set to work helping Pepper build the viewing platform for the top of the tower. Lily danced into the woods to gather more berries. "We need food to keep up our strength," she said.

Lily returned from her berry-gathering just as the platform was finished. Miles helped Pepper haul it to the top of the tower. Lily and Inch stayed at the bottom and held the tower steady. Then they all helped place the pole in the center, the pole that Inch and Lily would slide down when Inch spotted Ima Skunk.

"I need to go make a path through the meadow now," Miles said. He disappeared into the clover.

As the sun set and the full moon rose, Miles returned. Finally, the four workers had finished their jobs.

"Guess what, guys?" Miles said. "It took cooperation to build this tower. We all did our part."

"Right-o!" said Lily. "Now we can rest and eat these berries I gathered!"

That's when they smelled something.

"Skunk!" they all said at once.

Inch scrambled to the top of the tower where his binoculars were. When he reached the viewing platform, he searched the edge of the woods and the meadow for Ima Skunk. "I don't see her!" he called to the three at the base of the tower.

"Well, I smell skunk," Miles called back. "Keep looking! Lily, you better go up now. We don't want Inch falling asleep on the job."

"Right-o," said Lily. "I know the perfect song!"

"Just sing!" Pepper said. "Don't dance. We don't want the tower to fall again!"

"Right-o," said Lily, starting to climb the tower as Inch stood watch with his binoculars.

Miles picked up Lily's notebook. "Can I borrow this? Sketching will help me stay awake in the meadow."

"Sure," said Lily.

With Lily's notebook and his pencil box in hand, Miles waved good-bye to Pepper, who sat at the bottom of the tower. "See you later," he said, and ran to the path he'd made in the meadow.

The four friends were ready, each to do his or her part to keep Ima Skunk from stealing the bees' honey supply.

The moon rose higher and higher. Still no sign of Ima Skunk. The four friends waited, Miles in the meadow and Pepper at the base of the tower. Inch and Lily sat on the viewing platform. Inch kept watch with his binoculars. Lily sang to keep Inch awake. It was way past his bedtime. What would his mother think if she knew he was staying up all night?!

In the moonlit meadow, Miles sat waiting for Pepper. He picked up Lily's notebook and looked for a blank page. Then he began sketching pictures of their day in Beesville. He sketched building the watchtower. He sketched Pepper hanging and the tower tilting. He sketched Lily dancing, remembering to include the purple berry stains around her mouth.

Back at the tower, Lily stopped singing and yawned. Inch's eyelids felt very heavy. He couldn't keep them open. In a few moments, Lily and Inch were fast asleep at the top of the tower.

At the base of the tower, Pepper wondered, "Why did Lily stop singing?" He felt awfully sleepy. He closed his eyes. Soon he was snoring loudly.

Meanwhile, in the woods west of the

meadow, Ima Skunk was wide awake and very hungry! She foraged through the underbrush eating everything she could find—grubs, insects, and even a baby mouse. Then it was time for dessert. Ima had a sweet tooth and honey was her favorite! She had been waiting a whole month for the bees to fill up their honeycomb again with scrumptious, sweet honey! The full moon lit Ima's way across the wide meadow to where she knew the bees had their hive . . . and the honeycomb.

She hurried through the clover-filled meadow. And then something made her stop. Yum! A deliciously sweet smell was floating from . . . she sniffed again . . . high above. Yum! Whatever this sweet thing was, she had to have it!

Now!

CHAPTER 8

Skunk!

High on the watchtower, Inch awoke from a scary dream. He dreamed he saw his own face on a milk carton. But when he opened his eyes, he spied something even scarier. Ima Skunk! Ima was on the viewing platform squatting next to Lily, her nose stuck in Lily's lunch box!

Gently Inch nudged Lily awake. She rubbed her eyes. Inch nodded toward Ima, who was busy devouring the last of Lily's Twinkie. Lily's eyes got huge. Inch was afraid

Lily might scream . . . but she didn't. Quietly,
carefully, Inch and Lily tiptoed toward the
sliding pole and down they slid to the ground.

"Wake up!" Inch whispered, shaking Pepper. "She's here! Ima Skunk . . . up on the platform. Run! Tell Miles!"

Their plan had been foiled, but if Pepper ran fast, he still might be able to tell Miles about Ima. Then, if Miles ran fast enough, he could warn the bees that Ima Skunk was on her way.

Quickly Pepper disappeared into the path through the clover-filled meadow to find Miles.

"I'm coming too!" said Inch.

"Me too," said Lily.

As Inch and Lily took off behind Pepper, Inch looked up just in time to see something falling from the tower. "Watch out!" Inch said. Lily's lunch box crashed at their feet, nearly hitting Lily on the head.

Lily picked up her open lunch box and

shook it. "Empty," she sighed.

They looked up at the tower to see Ima sliding down the pole.

"Yikes! Let's go!" Inch said.

Lily reached into her pocket and pulled out a wrapped candy bar. She tossed it as far as she could toward the west. "Have a candy bar!" she called to Ima Skunk.

And then Lily took off down the meadow path just behind Inch. The candy bar, she hoped, would buy them all a little time. But would it be enough?

Time enough for Pepper to find Miles in the meadow?

Time enough for Miles to warn the bees?

Time enough for the bees to keep their honeycomb safe from Ima Skunk?

Time enough to save the colony?

CHAPTER 9

Heroes

As Lily ran down the meadow path, the one taken by Miles and then Pepper and then Inch, she kept looking back over her shoulder to see if Ima Skunk followed. Lily didn't see her. Maybe their plan would work, she thought.

After Lily reached the eastern border of the meadow where the woods began, she heard a strange sound. It was one she had never heard before, like the hum of a power saw. Close to the meadow's edge, she saw a small black cloud rising. The noise was coming from the cloud! As she got closer, she saw the cloud was really a swarm of bees, hundreds of them.

Inch, Miles, and Pepper came running out of the woods toward her.

"Hurry, Lily! Come into the woods where you'll be safe!" Miles called. "All the bees are ready now. Ready for Ima Skunk. We've done our part."

"We've cooperated," Inch said.

"Like Mr. Wooden told us," said Lily.

From their hiding place on a tree limb, Inch, Miles, Pepper, and Lily watched as hundreds of bees flew in from all over the meadow and surrounded the hive in one noisy, vibrating, swarming cloud. Their buzz was more of a roar, and their stingers were ready, ready for Ima Skunk. This time there would be no surprise attack, thanks to Inch, Miles, Pepper, and Lily. Cooperation had paid off.

"She's coming!" Miles said, staring through Inch's binoculars.

In a minute, with their very own eyes, all four friends could see Ima Skunk slinking through the meadow, sneaking ever closer to the hive.

Suddenly, the swarm swooped down, smack-dab in front of Ima, buzzing loudly. Ima stamped and hissed. Then she took one look at those hundreds of nasty stingers aimed at her and turned tail, shooting out a spray of stink as she raced off, but not before the swarm of bees shot high into the air, with Betty in the lead.

"Thanks, friends!" Betty called, waving at them. "You saved our colony. You're heroes! If you ever need anything from us bees, give a buzz!"

A package floated down with a little card
attached. Miles picked it up.

On the front of the card it said—

Beesville Honey Cooperative

Sweetest honey on Earth.

Made sweeter through cooperation.

Betty@beesville.com

Miles flipped the card over.

Work as one in all you do.

When you help others, they'll help you.

Seek to know what someone needs.

Then pitch right in and you'll succeed.

"Here, Lily," Miles said, handing her the package Betty had given them. "You open it."

"A piece of honeycomb!" Lily said. "Yum!"

"Well, guys," said Miles, holding the silver whistle up to his mouth. "I think the magic will work this time and get us back to school . . . now that we have what we came for."

"Honey?" asked Lily.

Inch laughed. "No, the block on the Pyramid of Success that will help us with our Open House project."

"And that block would be?" Pepper asked.

"Cooperation!" Inch and Miles shouted.

"Right-o," said Lily. "We did learn to cooperate. Now let's go home!"

EPILOGUE

Inch, Miles, Pepper, and Lily's Open House project earned them lots of applause from their families on Open House night . . . and, of course, a great deal of praise from their teacher, Mr. Wooden. Can you guess what their project was? A play, of course, entitled "The Heroes of Beesville." The play was written by Lily with help from Inch on the animal and bug research. The set was built by Pepper, with scenery and costumes designed by Miles. All four cooperated in the performance, including the singing, dancing, and acting. The hit song— "Wanna Be a Sensation? Try Cooperation!"— was the grand finale.

ABOUT THE AUTHORS

Coach and teacher **John Wooden** is a towering figure in 20th-century American sports. His UCLA basketball teams virtually created "March Madness" by amassing 10 national championships, 7 in a row; along with 4 perfect seasons; an 88-game winning streak; and 38 straight victories in tournament play.

Sports Illustrated says, "There has never been a finer man in American sports, or a finer coach."

Coach Wooden has two children, seven grandchildren, and eleven great-grandchildren.
(Visit CoachJohnWooden.com)

Steve Jamison is a best-selling author, award-winning television producer, and public speaker.
(Visit SteveJamison.com)

Bonnie Graves is the author of 13 books for young readers, both fiction and nonfiction. Beginning with *The Best Worst Day* in 1996, she has received several awards and honors for her work, including a 2005 South Carolina Children's Book Award nomination for her chapter book *Taking Care of Trouble.*